CYRIL PRICE'S LETTERS

Brian Radford

Published by New Generation Publishing in 2018

First Edition

www.newgeneration-publishing.com

 New Generation Publishing

THANKS:

I extend a very special 'thank you' to Emili, my multi-talented granddaughter, for her lively illustrations, and to Cyril Price, of course, without whom this book would never have been possible.

Diolch yn fawr!

BIOG:

Brian Radford is a freelance investigative journalist, who worked at the Western Mail in Cardiff for many years before moving to the Mirror Group offices in London.

A passionate Welshman from Gowerton, near Swansea, he has written 11 books, including ‘ghosted’ autobiographies of sports celebrities.

His most recent work was an amusing account of the daily life of the incomparable characters in Aber Tidy in Doolally Valley.

He is married to Jill, has a son, Toby, daughter Rebecca, and three grandchildren, Noah, Faye, and Emili.

Hobbies include an addiction to cricket, singing bass in male voice choirs, writing ‘fun’ tales, and staying in touch with his “wonderful” grandchildren.

He admits to possessing a bus pass!

………………

FRONT-COVER RAG-OUT QUOTES FROM LETTERS

"Cheap China steel has done immense damage to the industry in Wales, so well done on doubling their tariffs…"

TO PRESIDENT TRUMP

……………………………………………………………

"Your goons have been spraying Novichok on door handles, and storing it in perfume bottles. Please stop poisoning people."

TO PRESIDENT PUTIN

……………………………………………………………

"Our granddaughter, Gwenda, is seven today, and you're her hero. She dashes into my office and calls out, 'Boris, the lion, is on the tele!'"

TO BORIS JOHNSON

……………………………………………………………

"I was head judge, and I wore a bright red bowler, and Shirley, gasped, 'You're bleeding badly, boy! Get First Aid fast'"

TO SHIRLEY BASSEY

……………………………………………………………

"'Mandy, from Mumbles, will be assigned to Mr. Morgan. She specializes in stringing along money-grabbing rogues…'"

ABER TIDY DATING AGENCY

……………………………………………………………

"Eric is sure they weren't gnome-sick and gone back to Holland…"

ERIC SMITH'S THREE GNOMES DISAPPEAR

…………………………………………………………………

PLUS A FEW ADDRESSED ENVELOPES!

………………

CYRIL PRICE'S LETTERS

CYRIL Price was Aber Tidy's cheery postman for 30 years. He retired in December 2016 with ugly scars on both ankles, permanent reminders of where hungry dogs had sunk their teeth.

Though Cyril remains a big fan of most sports, he no longer participates, preferring to watch others use their energy on his 40-inch TV-set, with a glass of his favourite 'red' in one hand, and the channel changer in the other.

He desperately needed a hobby to fill his time, and to give him something purposeful to focus on. Having delivered letters all his life, he decided it was now his turn to write them, and for other people to deliver them.

Cyril regularly attends Sunday morning services at St. Mary's church, relishes expressing his opinion on any controversial topic, and now looks forward to writing to political leaders, celebrities in sport and entertainment, as well as people all over the Valley.

He is married to Joan, a retired history teacher, and currently lead soprano in the Aber Tidy Choral Society. They live at 12, Talbot Gardens, Aber Tidy, and they have two sons, one a lawyer in Spain, and the other a doctor in Singapore.

....

Cyril began his exciting new hobby on January 8, 2017.

....

ABER TIDY…was once a teeming mining town deep in Doolally Valley in South Wales.

Today, little remains of the vast pit that united a warm community, though the big wheel still stands proudly at the top of Bunker Hill, as a symbol of those bitterly hard days.

Way below it, you'll find chattering hotels and pubs, a small zoo, maternity clinic, three schools, four churches, three farms, a pickle factory, railway station, silver band, and enough wit and humour to cram its Ritz theatre every night of the week.

Sport thrives with a joint football and cricket club, along with competitive bowls, rugby, hockey, tennis, darts, cycling…

And enjoying it all is Cyril Price, the indefatigable 'scribbler', sending out prolific letters to help and advise, condemn and castigate, and always with an eye on putting the world to right…

Cyril will tell you, with a wink, of course, that in this case, it is one Price that is definitely right!

………………

HAPPY BIRTHDAY, SHIRLEY!

12, Albert Gardens,
Aber Tidy,
Doolally Valley,
South Wales.
January 8, 2017.

Janet Treasure,
Secretary,
Shirley Bassey Fan Club,
Goldfinger House,
Doolally Valley.

Dear Janet,

Please pass my best wishes to Shirley as she gracefully glides to her big 80!

Maybe she can remember me when she took time off from a week's gig at the Double Diamond Club in Caerphilly, and kindly opened the Aber Tidy annual Fruit and Veg show.

I was head judge that day, and wore a bright red bowler, and Shirley said, "You're bleeding badly, boy. Get First Aid fast!"

Daisy Lewis, a little lady with a squeaky voice, handed Shirley a huge hamper of fruit and veg after spilling half a glass of red wine down the front of her beautiful summer dress.

Shirley laughed it off, saying "Don't worry, love, I'll pick one up from Primark on the way home!"

Happy birthday! Happy memories!
Cyril Price (secretary Aber Tidy Fruit & Veg show)

12, Talbot Gardens,
Aber Tidy,
Doolally Valley,
South Wales.
February 19, 2017

Rev Gwyn Morgan,
St. Mary's Church,
Aber Tidy.

Dear Gwyn,

Joan and I are shocked and upset by what you said in the pulpit this morning about your affair with Debbie, our lovely young curate.

We have always admired you and Jenny, and your sporty 12-year-old twins, Dafydd and Hywel, who are so good at rugby.

They will miss you immensely. And we will miss you now that the Bishop has stopped you from officiating in any church, which is a terrible waste of leadership and talent.

We assume the lads will remain boarders at that high quality school in Sussex, which will help a lot.

Let us assure you that our friendship will not be affected by what has occurred, and we wish you all peace and understanding as your lives take a different route.

Yours in prayer,
Cyril and Joan

Reply from Rev. Gwyn Morgan

Croeso,
Trebanos Close,
Pontardawe.
February 23, 2017

Dear Cyril and Joan,

It was good to hear from you, and I'm sorry that things have worked out this way for our family.

Until everything settles down, I shall stay with my parents here in their bungalow in Pontardawe.

I intend to do lots of charity work, especially for Save the Children.

And I will go down to see the lads play rugby for the school's Under 15 team on Saturday mornings. They both play in the centre. They're strong, fast, and fearless.

You and I know each other very well, and trust each other, which is why I shall tell you something highly personal.

Hopefully, you will remember the Harvest Service when I arrived late, and with thick bandage wrapped around my head.

I raised a bit of a laugh when I said that I'd tripped over the neighbour's cat and struck my head against the garage wall.

Well, the truth is Jenny flipped when I dropped the sugar bowl onto the kitchen floor, and she banged me on the head with the frying-pan.

She can be really violent, and that's where Debbie stepped

in, helping me through the cuts and bruises, and it all went from there.

To be honest, I think Jenny's happier now without me, and I'm gladly free of all the mental and physical pain that she caused.

The lads know all about it, and fully understand, which is a terrific relief.

I'll definitely stay in touch.

May God be with you and Joan at all times.

Sincerely,
Gwyn.

12, Talbot Gardens,
Aber Tidy.
February 26, 2017.

Mrs. Megan Thomas,
Secretary,
Welsh Society,
Aber Tidy.

Dear Megan,

As you know the Rev. John Joseph is the principal guest at our annual St. David's Day dinner on March1, and I have written a tribute to him, referring to his days with us at St. Mary's, and his move to Sutton in Surrey.

Hope you like it.

Best wishes,
Cyril Price (chairman)

ODE TO BIG JOHN

It was late at night when the call came through,
A frantic voice saying, "We need you!"

"Whatever you're doing, you must put down,
And say you'll come to clean up our town."
It was Sheriff Sutton, Big John

He pulled on his boots, and hitched up his pants,
Looked in the mirror, and admired his stance.
Proud John

The clock on the wall kept ticking away,
There was no time to lose, he was going today.
Prompt John.

He collected his Bible and Common Prayer,
Emptied his pockets, and checked the fare.
Shrewd, Big John

He arrived at the station, loaded with bags,
A bottle of Scotch, and one or two gags!
The usual, Big John

Casey Jones he remembered well,
Stoking the boiler and ringing the bell.
Young days, Big John

He stormed into Sutton at the crack of dawn,
Satan was asleep, but not for long.
Beware, Big John

He strolled up the High Street just for a start,
And hitched a lift on the milkman's cart.
Weary, Big John?

The discos snored, the boozers were dead;
Sheriff Sutton was home in his bed.
Whacked out, Big John

He got off the cart down by the hall,
And read the graffiti on the wall
Educated, Big John

"Tell me, please, is it Tommy rot
that Karl Marx's grave was a Communist plot?"
That's clever, Big John

Sheriff Sutton, he crawled to the door,
A broken soul that could take no more.
Desperate, Big John

"Big John! Big John! Thank God you've come,
the sinners are winning ten-to-one!"
Like your horses, Big John

"Find those sinners, there must be chats,
let me convert them, dirty rats!"
That's Hollywood Big John

He asked for a gin to put him right
Before he went out to start the fight.
High Noon, Big John

History talks of many big names,
Wild Bill Hickok and Jesse James.
Now you, Big John

With cassock blowing in the wind,
The hunt was on for those who'd sinned.
Brave, Big John

"Hey, you there, Mr. Preacher man,
Would you like to join our Sutton gang?"
They're hoods, Big John

Clutching his Bible, he stood in the square,
Gamblers and drunkards, hundred were there.
Rum lot, Big John

Word went round that he'd come out of Wales,
A wizard in the valleys, or a deacon in the dales?
Got them guessing, Big John

From Fishguard, Tenby, Pantyffynon,
Penarth, Cardiff, Barry---John.

"Barry John!" went up the roar,
and you couldn't keep them back from the vestry door.
You've hooked them Big John!

The moral of this story is all about the toss,
About Sutton's gain, and Aber Tidy's loss.

Good men are not valued until they are gone.
So we welcome you back, our own Big John!

Thank you!

12, Talbot Gardens,
Aber Tidy,
Doolally Valley,
South Wales.
March 18, 2017.

Dear Linda,

As a close friend of Katherine Jenkins, please find a minute to read this plea.

My best friend, Morton, is devastated. He's Katherine's biggest fan in the world, and he's off his food, and hasn't slept for a week.

Nasty Nigel from Neath – Katherine's hometown – has rung him up, and said that he'd read that lovely Katherine had taken drugs when in university.

Morton went frantic, and wouldn't believe him. Then he checked on Google and saw it for himself.

He's so upset that he's used the 'f'' word for only the third time in his life. He did it when Dai 'twp' Richards ran over his foot, and when his wife caught him taking two chocolate fingers from the biscuit tin.

Please, please drop him a line through my address, above, to cheer him up, and call him Dynamite, it's his nickname. He'd love that.'

Best wishes,
Cyril Price

CEREAL OFFENDER

Cereal offender is facing 'porridge!'

Supt. Peter Matthews
Police Station,
Doolally Valley
April 5, 2017.

Good morning, Cyril,

We have a cereal offender in Aber Tidy, and I'd like your help. Two of my officers are on the case, but having no luck.

All supermarkets are on full alert, especially at the corn flakes shelves. Even with extra security staff, and Zach Jennings working a nine-hour shift, Tesco lost 35 packets last month, and 25 vanished at Sainsbury's.

Altogether 72 packets of corn flakes have been stolen from shops and supermarkets in the Valley in the past six weeks.

Very confidentially, we have our eye on Garfield Roberts, your close friend, and bowls club skipper, as he's shown up several times on CCTV near the corn flakes boxes in the Tesco store.

We are hoping you will do some undercover work for us, and try to get beyond his front door, and look around for clues.

Garfield is a huge Lego fan. His big hobby is piecing things together, and for several weeks cardboard cut-out cars have been on the back of corn flakes boxes. The cars are a red Ferrari, and sky blue Mercedes.

Good luck, and there's a drink on me at the Hare & Hounds if you pull it off.
Many thanks, Peter

12, Talbot Gardens,
Aber Tidy.
April 8, 2017

Hello Peter,

I called on Garfield yesterday, and I think the only cereal he can expect from now on is porridge!

He proudly showed me seven completed Mercedes, and he was assembling his sixth red Ferrari when I walked in. They'd all been cut from the back of corn flakes boxes.

Outside on the patio were two wheelbarrows full of corn flakes, and empty boxes galore, ready for a bonfire.

He put a finger to his lips when I asked if he had more to cut out.

So it's over to you. Not a word about me, but please keep me updated.

We'll miss him at the golf club!

Best wishes,
Cyril

HAIR RAISING SHOCK

Grass seed is root of hair-raising mystery!

Letter to hairdresser

12, Talbot Gardens
Aber Tidy.
April 15, 2017.

Manager,
Beyond the Fringe,
Men's hairdresser,
Gooseberry Street,
Aber Tidy.

Dear Manager,

Retired accountant Keith Andrew can't figure out why his hair is suddenly growing a lot faster than it's ever done before.

Since you opened in February, my good friend, Keith, says he's been back to you four times, which does seem a lot in ten weeks.

Keith is someone who never complains, which is why I'm contacting you on his behalf. To be honest, he's very suspicious of what might be going on at the salon.

He believes there's an ingredient in the water that is sprayed on his hair before it is cut that is causing it to grow so quickly.

Mike Harris and John Watts think the same as Keith, and would like Trading Standards to test the water.

Yours sincerely,
Cyril Price

Hairdresser's prompt reply

Beyond the Fringe,
Gooseberry Street,
Aber Tidy.
April 19, 2017.

Dear Mr. Price,

It's confession time. Keith, Mike, and John are correct. Their hair has grown three times quicker than ever before.

We apologise, and will refund the cost of two haircuts to everyone.

Selwyn, our new stylist, returned from holiday unaware that our rear lawn had been treated with a fast-growing seed to wake it up after the winter.

Unfortunately, the lawn specialist mixed the seed in the bowl we use for the water for our hair-spray bottles, and Selwyn innocently poured in every drop.

We've had a good laugh, and we hope our treasured customers will, too.

Before we discovered what had gone wrong, taxi boss, Morton Evans, had telephoned to say that his hair had gone green on one side, and we thought he had picked up some dye.

We are deeply sorry, and thank you so much for your continued custom.

Yours in the long grass,
Jill Wilson, manager

12, Talbot Gardens,
Aber Tidy,
May 8, 2017.

Manager,
Tesco store,
High Street,
Aber Tidy.

Dear manager,

My wife, Joan, and I, would like to congratulate Tesco for producing one of the tastiest Shepherd's Pie that we've ever had the pleasure to enjoy.

It was simply delicious, especially that smooth gravy that left us licking our lips like Chester, our marvelous ginger cat.

We also think that adding garden peas to the carrots was another big winner, and the mash was out of this world.

You beat everyone else by the proverbial mile. Well done! Take a bow!

Many thanks,
Cyril and Joan

Manager,
Tesco store,
High Street,
Aber Tidy.
May 15, 2017.

Dear Cyril and Joan,

Thank you so much for your kind words about the 'delicious' Shepherd's Pie, which I have passed on to the manager of Aldi. I regret that it was theirs not ours!

Ironically, their store is next door to Specsavers!

Anyway, thanks to you, we have now changed our gravy, and added garden peas to the carrots, which should make us more competitive.

Please find enclosed a voucher for £20, which you can use when you next visit our store.

We may even have our new Shepherd's Pie on sale by then.

Yours sincerely,
Mark Thorp
Store manager

12, Talbot Gardens,
Aber Tidy,
Doolally Valley.
June 5, 2017.

Matt Finish,
Painter & Decorator,
23, College Avenue,
Aber Tidy.

Dear Matt,

We arrived back from our Devon holiday just five minutes ago, and Joan and I are in deep shock.

Joan left a detailed list of what we wanted you to do, but you have not followed it one bit.

I am looking at the list right now. Joan asked for cream walls in the lounge to match our new leather suite, but the walls are a dull green, and the light blue we wanted in the hall is a bright red.

And none of the work we requested in the kitchen has been done. It's a complete shambles, and we paid you £1,500 in advance for a good job to be done.

Joan has gone to the bedroom, shaking in disbelief, and sobbing bitterly. How could it go so badly wrong?

Do please call in urgently so that we can discuss the best way forward.

Yours sincerely,
Cyril and Joan

23, College Avenue,
Aber Tidy,
June 7, 2017.

Dear Cyril and Joan,

I am very sorry about what has happened, and there is a clear explanation.

We took on Jacob from the Valley Youth Scheme to help us through the summer, and he confused our number12 with number 21, where we were doing identical work while Mr. and Mrs. Mitchell were in Scotland.

So, what they requested, you got, and they got what you requested.. The Mitchells are due home tomorrow.

All I can do is put everything right without delay, and I'll pay for a further week's holiday while we are doing the work.

We have now discovered that Jacob is dyslexic.

Best wishes,
Matt

HORSE WINS ON MARS BARS!

Hungry winner lands race on Mars!

12, Talbot Gardens,
Aber Tidy
June 18, 2017.

Lord Puffingdon,
Senior Steward,
Aber Tidy Jockey Club,
Epsom House,
Aber Tidy.

Dear Lord Puffingdon,

As head steward of the Aber Tidy racecourse meeting on April 15, I refer to winning hurdler Fingers Crossed, who later tested positive for a banned substance.

Laboratory technicians concluded that the stimulant came from at least one Mars bar, and probably two.

Fingers Crossed, outsider of 12 runners, won easily by six lengths, at vast odds of 150-1, and was winning for the first time in 82 races.

Baffled stewards ordered an immediate dope test, as the horse was so slow in its previous race that it finished just ahead of the ambulance.

Shocked trainer, Keith Hardman, told me: “I left two Mars bars and two packets of crisps near the horsebox rear door that were to be a snack for me and my assistant.

“But when I got back from buying a cup of tea, the Mars bars had gone, though the crisps were still there.

“I naturally assumed that a hungry stable-lad had taken them as he walked past. It never dawned on me that Fingers Crossed had eaten them.

"Obviously, when told that he had tested positive, I was mystified, as I knew that we had kept him strictly to his daily diet.

"Then, next day, the lad who looks after him, rushed into my office and said that he had found Mars wrappers in the horse's dung.

"I laughed for an hour. I couldn't believe he had been so greedy. One wasn't enough, he had to eat both."

Our investigators visited the Hardman stable and confirmed that Mars wrappers could be seen in the horse's waste.

A detailed report then went to our Turf Club's disciplinary committee in which the laboratory technicians said that the horse's urine sample contained theobromine, caffeine, and cocoa, and the committee accepted that the trainer could not be blamed.

Fingers Crossed was disqualified, and Ain't I Lucky promoted from second to first. The standard £5,000 fine was waived.

Very best wishes,
Cyril Price (Chief racecourse steward)

12, Talbot Gardens,
Aber Tidy.
June 27, 2017.

The manager,
Debbie's Dating Agency,
Doolally Valley.

Dear manager,

I know that you run a highly respectable, and confidential service.

However, I have good reason to believe that slippery Tommy Morgan, of Margam Road, has signed up with you, and is seeking a 'smart, intelligent lady in her late Forties with interests in healthy dining, movies, and walking'.

Well, if 'Tommy trouble' is on your books, and has listed those hobbies, let me warn you that he's a fraud.

Tommy has never walked farther than the betting shop, not seen a film since Roy Rogers and Trigger were rounding up the bad men, and does all his 'healthy' eating on greasy burghers in Jackie's Den.

He's also married with two teenage sons, is 53, not 38, and pockets a weekly windfall from every State Benefit the Government can offer.

But he's a charmer, and even the sharpest female brain finds it impossible to resist his sweet-talk, and happily 'lend' him thousands of pounds to help fund his mysterious top-secret project, which is total nonsense.

In strictest confidence, Cyril Price

Debbie's Dating Agency,
Doolally Valley.
June 30, 2017.

Dear Mr. Price,

Strict data Protection regulations prevent us from discussing our clients, but we can confirm that Mr. Tommy Morgan is registered with us.

Should your advice on Mr. Morgan be true, we have specially trained ladies to escort that type of male client.

Mandy from Mumbles will be assigned to Mr. Morgan. She specializes in stringing along money-seeking rogues. She's tall and elegant, and will dazzle him with her personality, which matches her flaming red hair.

She will talk about her Ferrari back in Italy for its annual MOT, her three racehorses, and her £200,000 yacht in Cardiff marina.

Truth is, she drives a ten-year-old VW Beetle, wouldn't know which end of a horse eats, and spends weekends on her kayak in the Vale of Glamorgan.

And she never fails to carry a well-hidden tape-recorder, so it should be fun!

Thank you for contacting us, and should you ever feel lonely and lost, we'll find someone nice to keep you company, and with no charge.

Love. Kathy Seymour,
Manager, Debbie's Dating Agency
xxx

12, Talbot Gardens,
Aber Tidy,
Doolally Valley,
South Wales.
July 13, 2017.

Andy Murray,
Tennis ace,
c/o Wimbledon office,
Wimbledon.

Dear Andy,

Along with millions in the country, I am deeply disappointed that your terrible hip problem caused you to lose in the recent Wimbledon quarter-finals.

However, despite the defeat, you managed to smile three times in the four-minute television interview about the match and your injury.

This was great for me, as I have a running bet with Marcel, the French chef at The Bell, who says you never smile, even when you win.

Well, I've taken him on, and every time you smile I pick up £25 and a three-course meal, but if you remain morose, as you can do, then I pay him £25 and the cost of the meal.

So please think of me in all future TV interviews, and good luck in sorting out the hip.

Best wishes,
Cyril Price (former Aber Tidy singles champion)

Anthony Bassett,
Area Manager,
BT Communications,
Cable House,
Aber Tidy.
July 25, 2017.

Dear Mr. Price,

I refer to your complaint regarding repeated nuisance calls from people with Asian accents.

Please tape-record the next one, and send me a copy so that I can try to locate the caller.

Thank you,

Yours sincerely,
Anthony Bassett
Area manager.

12, Talbot Gardens,
Aber Tidy.
July 30, 2017.

Dear Mr. Bassett,

Thank you for your advice. I am adding to this email the transcript of a tape-recording of a conversation with a man with an Asian accent, who said he was Sam.

Yours sincerely,
Cyril Price

TRANSCRIPT

Caller: Me Sam. Me warn if you not press
5 on phone now, you computer shut down in next hour.

Cyril: Wow!

Caller: You Mr. Price?

Cyril: No, me Half Price.

Caller: You Half Price, yes?

Cyril: And my wife, she is Half Price, and when we're together, we're Full Price.

Caller: Me confused.

Cyril: And when I sliced my finger with a knife last week, I was Cut Price.

Caller: Me very confused. You Full Price, Half Price, and now Cut Price.

Cyril: Sam, you have same voice as David, who called yesterday.

Caller: Yes, me David yesterday, and Thomas tomorrow. And I use same voice.

Cyril: Thank you.

Caller: You want Thomas to call you tomorrow?

Cyril: No! No! Not at any price.

Caller: Who N.E.Price? Me speak to N.E. Price, yes?

Cyril: I had to put the phone down.

End of transcript.

Thank you.

Cyril Price

+ Dai 'twp' Richards has also reported receiving nuisance calls from a G.Raff. Supt. Matthews has traced them to a phone-box outside the zoo, and quickly ruled out Eddie, the elephant, as they weren't trunk calls!

Aber Tidy FC/Cricket Club,
Boundary Lane,
Aber Tidy.
August 5, 2017.

Dear Cyril,

Our popular goalkeeper, and wicket-keeper, Terry Jenkins, has decided to retire from all active sport from today.

Of course, you will know him as ‘Butterfingers Jenkins’.

He’ll be greatly missed, particularly by our opponents, and especially Black Mountain Rangers, who put 20 past him in three matches in a row.

For his unbroken loyalty over 22 years, both of our clubs are arranging a special ‘thank you’ evening of entertainment, and tributes, at the town hall on August 25, so please put that in your diary now.

More information will be sent out in the next few days.

In the meantime, why not contact him with your own thanks and best wishes.

Yours sincerely,
Joe Grierson,
Vice Chairman Aber Tidy FC

12, Talbot Gardens,
Aber Tidy.
August 8, 2017.

Dear Terry,

Club vice chairman, Joe Grierson, is emailing members of our two clubs with news that you are quitting football and cricket, as from today.

Saturdays will never be the same. My friends would say "I'm off to the match!" but I always said, "I'm off to see Butterfingers", not knowing what to expect.

Do you remember the match against Black Mountain Rangers when that enormous wind was blowing down the pitch and their keeper scored three goals in ten minutes, as the ball kept bouncing over your head? We lost 19-1.

And what about the day you saved a penalty against Sugarloaf Rovers when the taker thumped the ball so hard it struck you smack in the face, and flew over the bar, and you were stretched off.

And I'll never forget you playing against Wilson Avenue Hackers when Spanish striker, Swan Vesta, who always lit up a match, sliced his shot, and the ball struck the ref on the back of the head and soared into the top corner.

Many thanks for so many terrific days, and be assured your League record of conceding 134 goals in one season will never be broken, nor will your 22 dropped catches, and 15 missed stumpings in summer 2014.

Best wishes,
Cyril (Price)

Letter to traffic manager

12, Talbot Gardens,
Aber Tidy.
August 15, 2017.

Thomas Thomas,
Manager,
Traffic Department,
Council Offices,
Aber Tidy.

Hi Tommy,

Picking up on our chat at bowls last week (how's the lumbago?) five shops have been forced to close in Palace Road in the past nine months, and four more in the Tawe Centre.

Several others are struggling, and look sure to shut soon unless the council can rescue them.

I have no doubt that council car parking charges are to blame for keeping potential shoppers away, and this is having a devastating affect.

Shoppers won't pay £3.00 an hour in the multi-storey, and certainly not £3.50 in the town centre.

Please bring down these stupidly inflated charges to halt the exodus, and help those battling to survive.

Best wishes,
Cyril

Traffic manager,
Aber Tidy Council
August 17, 2017.

Nice one, Cyril!

You make me sound like Jesse James with his posse waiting to ambush the Deadwood Stage.

You can expect a big cut in parking fees, starting next month.

Seriously, you have a very good point, and I'm already speaking to Sheriff Sharples (CEO) about it.

Must dash, I see the Deadwood Stage is comin' on over the hill headed by the Man from Larami (Dai Jones, Admin).

See you at bowls on Thursday. Back is a lot better.

Best wishes,
Tommy (Tonto) Thomas

LAND DETECTOR UNEARTHS RARE COINS

Land detector unearths rare coins

Daffodil House,
Long Lane,
Aber Tidy.
August 26, 2017.

Dear Cyril,

We have a crisis. Lucy's lost her wedding ring. We've hunted high and low through the house, garden, and car, but all in vain.

Lucy now thinks it might have slipped off while picking blackberries on the common last week.

So we're desperately hoping you will lend us your metal detector, and we'll search the blackberry bushes we went to.

Please don't write back, just ring and let me know that I can borrow it, and I'll arrange to call in.

We've put an advert in The Gazette's 'lost and found' and tied a few posters to lampposts.

Many thanks,
Trevor and Lucy

Daffodil House,
Long Lane,
Aber Tidy.
September 2, 2017.

Hi Cyril,

Eureka! We're so excited. We've struck gold! Well, virtually.

Your detector picked up two very rare Anglo Saxon coins as we walked across the common. We went straight to Sue Bennett at the museum, who valued them at £5,000 each. Sue's our leading marathon runner.

We were so shocked that we almost forgot that we were there to look for Lucy's wedding ring. And we found it.

We had gone to every blackberry bush, and were on our way home when Lucy stopped at the stream to wash her hands, just as she did after picking the blackberries, and there, right under her nose, stuck between two large stones, was the ring.

I've just splashed £185.00 on a smart detector, and I'm hoping we can comb the common together, and become rich…

Can't think of a better hobby. How about it? Why not ring me and say 'yes'?

Again, many thanks. Drinks are on me!

Best wishes,
Trevor and Lucy

Letter to Hilda Hopkins

12, Talbot Gardens,
Aber Tidy,
Doolally Valley.
September 4, 2017

Dear Mrs. Hopkins,

I hope you don't mind, but I offered some friendly advice to your son, Gavin, earlier today. I believe he's nine now.

He was smoking a cigarette behind the bowls club pavilion, and was preparing to drink from a bottle of beer.

He was very polite, and seemed to accept what I said about cigarettes and alcohol being bad for his health.

What really worried me was that he said you had bought the cigarettes and beer for him in the supermarket. Could this be true?

He said that you allowed him to smoke five cigarettes a day, and drink ten bottles of beer a week, which must be wrong for someone so young.

Best wishes,
Cyril Price

BOY, 9, IN DRINK AND DRUGS BATTLE

Gavin, 9, battles against booze and drugs

Hilda Hopkins reply

18, Victoria Road,
Aber Tidy,
September 8, 2017.

Dear Mr. Price,

Please mind your own business if you want to stay in one piece. Just keep your big nose out of other people's private affairs!

If you really must know, we are desperately trying to get Gavin off cocaine and gin, so I leave beer and fags in the shed for him to pick up when he gets back from school.

His 18-year-old brother, Luke, comes out of nick next week after doing two years for selling cheap coke at the secondary school.

Their dad is also due out in a month, having done his three years for drink, drugs, and affray, so we'll all be here to help Gavin.

We know what to do. So stay away.

Thank you,
Hilda Hopkins and family

12, Talbot Gardens,
Aber Tidy
October 4, 2017

Editor,
Aber Tidy Gazette,
Print House,
Station Road,
Aber Tidy.

Dear Mr. Editor,

Two of our popular town councillors were happy to chat with me in The Bell last week about the opportunity they get to make a lot of money from business people all over the Valley.

They spoke freely about 'big bungs' from companies and private businesses, and literally laughed when I said they'd need to be careful not to get caught.

"Evidence, Cyril," one of them said. "They'd need evidence."

I said that someone might get a whisper of what was going on, and tell the Gazette's editor, and they laughed even louder.

"He's well looked after," said Mr. Talkalot, and you'll know who that was!

They also challenged me to tell you that you had 'history', and that you wouldn't publish anything bad about them or they'd blow the big whistle.

Not nice, even if a rotten joke.

Yours sincerely, Cyril Price

Editor's reply

Aber Tidy Gazette,
Print House,
Aber Tidy.
18th October, 2017.

Dear Mr. Price,

Be honest, what would you do if you had a £50,000 gambling debt, drank a bottle of Scotch every evening, and drove a 25-year-old battered banger?

So it's just as well that I've never had a bet in my life, only drink a couple of lagers at the weekend, and drive a smart BMW with just 8,000 miles on the clock.

Anyway, many thanks for the idea, and do please confirm names of the two councillors so that I can offer my services.

Yours sincerely,
Andy Lloyd
Editor

MARTHA, 94, CELEBRATES WITH DRIVE TO PARIS

Ooo, la, la, Martha, 94, in dramatic drive to Paris

Letter to Martha Davies

12, Talbot Gardens,
Aber Tidy.
October 24, 2017.

Dear Martha,

Everyone at the Bridge Club congratulates you on reaching a fabulous 94! Brilliant!

However, we are deeply concerned that you are still driving on our dangerous roads, and putting yourself at great risk.

I must mention that Peggy Potts was in deep shock at Bridge yesterday while telling us that you came within a whisker of knocking her down on the crossing outside the primary school.

Three times she dropped her cards, and the Jack of Hearts got drenched when it fell into her cup of tea.

Your lovely neighbour, Pam Harrison, is also worried after watching you trying to start your car from the passenger's seat, and getting angry when you couldn't find the steering-wheel.

You were obviously badly confused, and on behalf of every pedestrian in Aber Tidy, we all ask you to think seriously of handing in your licence.

Meanwhile, enjoy a memorable birthday!

Best wishes,
Cyril (Price, secretary) and everyone at our Bridge Club

Martha Davies reply

Willow Cottage,
Fairwood,
Aber Tidy.
October 28, 2017.

Dear Mr Price and Bridge players,

I have driven cars for more than 70 years and I don't see why I should stop now, especially as there is still a lot of Europe I would like to visit in my amazingly reliable 1964 Morris Minor.

In fact, my young sister, Brenda, who's 88 in January, is joining me next month on a journey to Paris, which has always been my dream.

Brenda will be my navigator, though she depends a lot on her magnifying glass now, but we'll manage.

I can't wait to see the Tower, and drive around the Arc de Triomphe, which should be fun.

Brenda keeps telling me that I must remember to drive on the right-hand side of the road, and I'm hoping my arthritis will be fine, as I can barely turn the wheel when it's bad.

Please let me know if anyone at the Bridge Club would like to come with us. We plan to go in mid-December.

Very best wishes,
Martha (Aber Tidy's answer to Lewis Hamilton!)

12, Talbot Gardens,
Aber Tidy.
December 10, 2017

Supt. Matthews,
Aber Tidy Police,
Doolally Headquarters,
Station Road,
Aber Tidy.

Dear Peter,

With Christmas just two weeks away, I am worried that the present high number of burglaries will get even worse when homes are left unattended while people are out celebrating the Festive season.

Is there anything that you can tell me, confidentially, that you are doing to help us protect our property and valuables, which can put my mind at rest?

As you can imagine, Joan is terrified that we'll be added to the 25 local homes that have been robbed in the past six months.

She is so paranoid that we're going to be the next, that she's put all her jewellery in a safe box under the stairs, and is thinking of buying a guard dog!

Hoping for the best.

Cheers,
Cyril

Supt. Matthews reply

Aber Tidy Police,
Doolally Headquarters
Station Road,
Aber Tidy.
December 17, 2017

Dear Cyril,

I understand your concern, but do please tell Joan that we have a strategy to deal with these robbers over Christmas. I will tell you in strict confidence.

We have assembled a Santa Squad of five officers who will wear full Father Christmas outfits, and walk the streets through the day and night.

The Gazette will run a story tomorrow disclosing what we're doing, and making it seem that it's being done to entertain the children.

Any sign of a robbery, and the officers will rip off their Santa disguise and fly into action. As you can guess, it's needed a new Claus in their contract!

Best wishes to Joan

See you at the bowls club dinner on Tuesday.

Peter

12, Talbot Gardens,
Aber Tidy.
January 6, 2018.

Mrs. Kathryn Harris,
Director,
Crown Homes,
Jesmond Avenue,
Aber Tidy.

Dear Kath,

The shock news has just reached me that 35 elderly people at the Homes had their dentures stolen while they slept last night.

According to manager, Stuart Atkinson, they were taken from glass jars on bedside tables.

Stuart also said that Supt. Matthews told him that simultaneous raids were carried out on other Homes in Doolally Valley.

He believes the dentures would have been placed in large, secure bags, driven to a UK port, and shipped abroad, ending up in Asia, where they would fetch big money on the black market.

In all the gloom, he couldn't resist saying that Annie Green's bark would be far worse than her bite!

Do let me know if I can be of any help.

Best wishes,
Cyril

Crown Homes,
Jesmond Avenue,
Aber Tidy.
January 8, 2018.

Dear Cyril,

Thank you for writing to me on this dreadful occasion. Everyone is distraught, mystified, and very hungry!

Police chief Matthews and two officers have been here all day, along with Forensic people looking for fingerprints, and other clues.

Supt. Matthews said four Homes were hit, and more than 200 dentures were taken, as well as lots of spectacles, and hearing aids.

We've had very elderly people who couldn't eat, see or hear. It's been quite desperate.

At first, we thought it was the denture factory staff who've been fighting tooth and nail to keep their jobs as business is so bad.

Police were called to the Homes after the dentures were found in buckets in a warehouse marked up for Asia.

Annie Lewis, aged 89, had struck 88-year-old Maggie Jones with her walking-stick while insisting that she had her beautiful set of dentures, and the 'wobbly rubbish' she had been given belonged to Oscar Morgan, who desperately needed them for the Victoria Sponge on his 92nd birthday. Supt. Matthews said: "No comment just yet. We've got a lot to chew over!"

I'll keep you informed.
Best wishes, Kath

12, Talbot Gardens,
Aber Tidy.
January 14, 2018.

Mansel Thomas,
Chairman,
Town Council,
Market Square,
Aber Tidy.

Dear Mansel,

As you know, work has come to a halt at the council-owned pickle factory and, as a senior adviser responsible for production, I require your immediate assistance to put things right.

Works manager, Pamela Harrison, has reported that the 20 cases of onions recently bought in France – Normandy, I believe - are far too big for our production-line grabbers, and too big for the jars in which they are sold.

We aim to place a minimum of 12 onions in each jar, but we can manage only five with this lot.

All 40 staff, which includes management, have left the building, as no work can be done until a new supply arrives.

Please keep me updated.

Many thanks,
Cyril

Council Offices,
Broadway,
Aber Tidy.
January 17, 2018.

Dear Cyril,

What a pickle at the pickle factory.

It's just as well that Pam Harrison had second thoughts about retiring and is still in charge. She certainly knows her onions!

At one stage, we were worried that daffodil bulbs had been sent to us in error.

Anisa Swails is speaking to our French suppliers right now and seeking a little compensation.

A special delivery is being swiftly arranged, so you should be able to restart in two to three days.

To throw away such healthy onions brings tears to my eyes, so we're keeping a dozen for a few bowls of soup. Do let me know if Joan would like some.

Sorry about the problem, which will be fully investigated.

Best wishes,
Mansel

12, Talbot Gardens,
Aber Tidy,
January 26, 2018

Blodwen Morgan,
Chairman,
Neighbourhood Watch,
17, Goldwell Drive,
Aber Tidy.

Dear Blodwen,

Ron and Sheila Harris have just rung me with the shocking news that they've been robbed by a conman calling himself Jimmy Gray.

Can you please flash an urgent warning to all your contacts, including the Gazette, and I will notify Supt. Matthews to put out a description of this crook.

Ron has told me it all began in Tesco car park one day last week when this chap came up and offered to help Sheila put her grocery bags in the car.

He said he had just moved into Aber Tidy and was a bit lonely, so Sheila invited him back for a chat and a cuppa, and he said he was a retired Met Police officer, who protected the royals.

He was absolutely charming. Then two days later he called at the house with two free tickets for the opera at the town hall. Ron and Sheila were delighted and he stayed for another long chat.

He said he was in lodgings without a TV and there was a big football match being shown on the opera night, and he was going to try to find somewhere to watch it.

Ron and Sheila jumped at the chance to show their gratitude, and invited him to watch the match on their TV, and made a meal for him before they left for the opera.

They returned home at 10.30 pm and, though every light in the house was switched on, there was no sign of their friend.

He had gone, and taken all Sheila's expensive jewellery with him, as well as £850 they had tucked into a bedroom drawer that was to be a deposit on a month's holiday in Greece.

Please contact Ron and Sheila on Aber Tidy 33900. I shall speak to Supt Matthews shortly, and I'm sure he'll ask an officer to go round quickly and get a detailed description of this conman.

Best wishes,
Cyril (Price)

Police Station,
Aber Tidy.
February 3, 2018.

Dear Cyril,

Thank you for contacting Mrs. Blodwen Morgan, at Neighbourhood Watch, about the shocking conman who robbed Ron and Sheila Harris.

Police Forces all over the UK are aware of this rogue, who has many aliases, and many disguises.

On one occasion he pretended to be a blind man, tapping the streets with a white stick, while begging in the North-East of England.

Probably his worst trick is sitting in hospital waiting-rooms. and telling visitors who have travelled a long distance that he has a 'spare' apartment just 100 yards away where they can stay the night for just £50.

He then hands over a key, but when they reach the address, they find there's no apartment. They've been callously robbed.

It's difficult to put out a positive description because of his many disguises, but I think we're closing in.

I'll keep you informed.

Thanks again,

Peter

12, Talbot Gardens,
Aber Tidy.
February 17, 2018.

Supt Matthews,
Police Station,
Aber Tidy.

Dear Peter,

I've just heard from Lukas at Fred's Fish Bar that he's been arrested as an illegal immigrant, and he's being sent back to Poland.

Is there anything you can do to stop this from happening? It's an absolute hammer blow to Joan and me.

Just between us, Lukas always gives me a double portion of chips, picks out the best fish for Joan, and makes sure I get the largest faggots with lots of peas.

On top of that, he cuts my hair, mows the lawn, cleans the windows, and washes both cars every Sunday afternoon, and all it costs us is £20 for the lot.

Please do your best to keep him here.

Good luck!
Cyril

Police Station,
Aber Tidy.
February, 2018.

Dear Cyril,

Believe me, I am doing all I can to convince the Home Office that Lukas is a hard worker, and not one of those who's here to milk the State.

What's more, and just between us, I'll find it very difficult to manage without him. He cuts my lawns, trims the hedges, does our big Tesco shopping twice a week, cleans the cars, and is a great handyman.

No matter whether it's a plumbing problem, trouble with the electrics, painting and decorating, Lukas will do a professional job at half the price of anyone in the town.

Best of all, his close friend's brother plays rugby for Wales, and he always gets a ticket for me for the big international matches.

I'm doing everything I can to keep him in the UK, and I shall tell a few politicians it's payback time for all the favours I've done for them, especially with their driving licences.

The media would have a field day if I blew the whistle, so I'm very hopeful that our wonderful Man Friday won't be going anywhere.

Best wishes,
Peter

12, Talbot Gardens,
Aber Tidy.
March 9, 2018.

Mrs. Peggy Phillips,
Secretary,
Aber Tidy Bird Club,
Eagle House,
Aber Tidy.

Dear Peggy,

Thank you for writing to me. Yes, I was aware that our internationally-renown birdman, Professor Sam Sparrow, has flown.

There seems little doubt that it follows his mistaking an overfed Red Kite for the rare Red-crowned Crane, usually found in East Asia, more than 4,000 miles away.

From what you say, it seems Prof. Sparrow was so sure it was a Red-crowned Crane that he spread it all over social media, which explains why Aber Tidy is suddenly crammed with cameras and video equipment.

Chartered coaches have arrived from as far as Scotland and Cornwall, and all our hotels and guesthouses are booked up, and tents and caravans are filling our fields.

Meanwhile, I understand Prof. Sparrow has been seen up a tree in the Brecon Beacons.

Of course, our struggling traders see him as a hero, especially hotels and cafes, and taxi boss, Morton Evans, who's done so well that he's paying for a two-week cruise for his wife, Marcella, and her friend, Jill.

I see that Mrs. Freda Sparrow has spoken to The Gazette, who quoted her saying, "It seems Sam has ruffled a few feathers.

"For a few days he'd complained that his new specs were not quite right, and I told him not to flap. Everyone makes a mistake. It's not murder."

I'm now being told that Ying Tong, the Beijing birdman, wandered into the square as it was getting dark, and pointed to the town hall roof, and called out, "That velly rare bird! That velly rare!"

Within minutes hundreds of cameras clicked, bulbs flashed, and mature birdmen crowed hysterically. They had never seen anything like it before. It had a big head, big breast, a broad rear end, and was grey all over.

As they excitedly guessed what it was, Prof. Sparrow flew in, settled on the town hall steps, grabbed a loud-speaker, and addressed the crowd.

He began: "Yes, you're right, it's unique. It's the only one of its kind in the world."

Loud gasps of delight drowned the cameras as they clicked even more. It was the best day of their lives.

Prof. Sparrow didn't have the heart to tell them it was an ordinary lump of lead shaped by Port Talbot steelworker, John Morris, and had been the town's weathervane for more than 40 years.

Instead, he flew back to the Beacons in a three-wheeler Robin before daylight revealed the shocking truth.

Best wishes, Cyril

12, Talbot Gardens,
Aber Tidy,
March 21, 2018.

Oliver Williams,
Musical director,
Doolally Valley Concert Band

Dear Oliver,

We have been close friends for more than 30 years, and I just cannot believe that you've breached our deep musical trust by poaching the hugely talented Glyn Evans from the Aber Tidy Silver Band, of which I am president, as you know.

Glyn has been with us since the age of ten, and we've invested a lot of money in having him coached by the very best trombonists.

Now, at 25, he is at his peak. He was our prime soloist. He leaves a massive gap that will badly affect our chance of defending the Valley Band of the Year title in June.

A reliable 'mole' has said that you tempted him away with a deposit for a car, now that he's passed his test, and a new washing-machine for his mother.

Please deny if untrue.

I shall speak to Glyn when the opportunity arises, but I shall not dare invite him back. In any case, we don't have the money for a car or a washing-machine for Maggie! So he's all yours.

Cyril

Strike Up!
Clifford Close,
Aber Tidy.
April 6, 2018,

Hi Cyril,

Calm down, boy, calm down!

To be completely accurate the money we gave Glyn was a loan, and it was a dishwasher, not a washing-machine.

Glyn would have joined us, anyway, without all these perks, as his biggest perk is in the trumpet section, the lovely Jenny Howells, whom he's been dating for a few months.

And you're making such a big fuss, as though it's something you've never done. You certainly found a sponsor to get Harry Lester from us, and Jack Morris from the Doolally Drifters.

If Glyn is happy to play with the Silver Band in the crucial competition coming up, I certainly wouldn't stand in his way.

Why don't the three of us meet for a coffee and chat in Dina's and talk it through. I'll speak to Glyn and find the most convenient day and time.

Let me know how you feel about that.

Best wishes,
Oliver

12, Talbot Gardens,
Aber Tidy,
Doolally Valley,
May 6, 2018.

Mansel Thomas,
Chairman,
Town Council,
Aber Tidy.

Dear Mansel,

Thank you for letting me know about the proposed Gee-Cee massage parlour in Clifton Street, which sounds extremely interesting, not that I'll be a member like Dai 'twp' Richards, Tommy Morgan, and Johnny 'muscles' Morris.

However, I might pop in under a false name to test their technique, and give marks out of ten, though I'd end up under the patio if Joan found out.

From their CVs, the owners look a highly respectable and competent couple, which is imperative in such a controversial business.

Both Georgina and Caroline (Gee-Cee) are joining forces as good friends, who will remain in the nursing profession, while finding time to manage the business and, maybe, recruit a couple of assistants, though I'd be totally against anyone from Thailand bringing in their exotic stuff.

My cousin, Colin, from Carmarthen, brought a girl home from Bangkok, who turned out to be a Thai Kick-boxer, and she beat him up, and she'd worked in a massage parlour.

I can’t imagine our Georgina and Caroline being kick-boxers, can you? But, I suppose, we should check, especially Caroline, who’s quite nifty on her feet.

The parlour is right next door to Ladbrokes’ betting shop, so the three who work there, Damien, Ian and Marco are guaranteed to be regulars, particularly Damien who needs a flexi arm and shoulder for his darts.

Call him ‘double top’ and they’ll land a nice tip. He really likes being called ‘double top’.

Please ensure strict rules are applied to all clients, especially no entry to anyone over 85 with a pacemaker.

You ask me about them being allowed to beat clients with bamboo sticks, Turkish style, and I think that’s fine, but with extreme care not to cause any testicular damage.

So, we’ve got exciting times ahead. Catch up at Thursday’s meeting.

Best wishes, Cyril

12, Talbot Gardens,
Aber Tidy.
May 15, 2018.

Nicole,
Entertainments Office,
Town Council,
Aber Tidy.

Hi Nicole,

From votes cast so far it seems that marathon champions Sue and Anthea are going to run away with this year's Doolally Valley's top sports award.

Kayak duo, Pete and Di (Di-namite to friends), are making a late splash, but I think there's far too much water to make up.

Voting closes on May 23, and the awards will be presented at the Town Hall on June 9. We were going to ask 'Butterfingers' Jenkins to do the honours, but the committee now fears he could drop the trophy, and cost us a packet.

It will probably be Austin Keep, from the cricket club, provided he can get the night off.

I understand you are filling in there while studying journalism at Bournemouth University, which is good experience.

Best wishes,
Cyril Price (sports awards organizer)

Letter to President Putin

12, Talbot Gardens,
Aber Tidy,
Doolally Valley,
South Wales.
July 11, 2018.

President Putin,
Kremlin,
Moscow,
Russia.

Dear President Putin,

Please stop poisoning people in Salisbury, which is less than 100 miles from me, here in Aber Tidy.

Your deadly nerve agent Novichok has already killed one innocent lady, and others have been critically ill, but are now fit again, and left hospital.

Your goons have been spraying Novichok on door handles, and storing it up in perfume bottles.

My granddad, Sam, read the Morning Star for many years to get the Communist news and views.

Our family understands your ambition to rule the world, and your political power to do it.

But, please, no more Novichok!

Thank you very much.

Cyril Price

12, Talbot Gardens,
Aber Tidy,
July 30, 2018.

Angie Thorp,
Secretary,
Cliff's Fan Club (Doolally),
Groveland Road,
Aber Tidy.

Hi Angie,

Please say 'well done' to Cliff on beating those BBC clowns, and if he's got a few pounds to spare from his windfall, we'd really appreciate a donation at the bowls club, as the pavilion desperately needs a new roof.

Please ask Cliff how much he remembers of his hilarious night at the Aber Tidy Conservative Club in the Eighties when he won a tin of cream rice for having a full line on our bingo. He shared top-of-the-bill with 'Rita the fire-eater' from Resolven.

There was so much smoke we could hardly see him on stage, but he sang beautifully, and took requests.

Peggy Matthews, a Sunday School teacher, asked for Calon Lan, a hugely popular Welsh hymn, which left Cliff speechless, though he did smile when Joe 'Dipstick' , the mechanic, dropped a full tray of drinks while Cliff was singing 'Congratulations', which got a huge laugh.

For a joke, please tell Cliff that our new ballad singer, Rocky Hughes, has brought out a disc that has 'I love you' on the 'A' side, and 'Kiss Me' on the back side.

Best wishes,
Cyril

12, Talbot Gardens,
Aber Tidy,
Doolally Valley,
South Wales, UK,
August 2, 2018.

President Trump,
White House,
Washington,
United States.

Dear President Trump,

Dai Morgan and I think you are doing a great job, especially with those hefty new tariff charges to protect the United States workforce.

Cheap China steel has done immense damage to the industry in South Wales, with orders drying up all over the world, so well done on doubling their tariffs on steel and aluminium.

Congratulations on putting the United States first in everything you do while battling for jobs and prosperity, which was the main thrust of your election promises.

Keep up the good work, and don't worry about all those sleaze stories, as you're not a patch on Arthur Howells, of Elba Street, who's got four children by four different women, including one in Belfast.

Best wishes,
Cyril Price and Dai Morgan

Letter to Geraint Thomas, winner of Tour de France

12, Talbot Gardens,
Aber Tidy.
August 7, 2018.

Dear Geraint,

Congratulations! Terrific result! And if you can believe Ted Lewis, night manager at The Bell Hotel, you are one of us, an Aber Tidy 'seed'.

Let me explain. Ted has put it around that your parents, Howell and Hilary, spent two nights in room 25, exactly nine months before you came into the world.

He's adamant that they stayed there in August 1985, and you, of course, were born in May 1986.

Guests and visitors are paying £2 to enter room 25, where they can photograph and video-record all that's there. Ted says every penny will go to charity, and jokes that no-one is being taken for a ride!

Should you ever have the time, do please call to see us, and I guarantee that you won't be charged a penny if you pop into room 25!

What a great picture that would make!

Yours sincerely,
Cyril Price

Letter to Boris Johnson

12, Talbot Gardens,
Aber Tidy,
Doolally Valley,
South Wales
August 8, 2018.

Boris Johnson MP,
House of Commons,
London.

Dear Boris,

Whatever you think of the burkha, we could do with two here in Aber Tidy.

One, to cover up Alice in Donkey Street, and another to slap on grisly Gaynor, a real horse lookalike---big nose, big teeth, big tongue.

On a brighter note, our bubbly granddaughter, Gwenda, is seven today, and you're her hero!

She'll dart into my office calling out, "Boris, the lion, is on the tele." It must be your mane, that unique hairstyle.

I've been a Labour man all my life, but I do admire your honesty and feisty energy.

It would be great if you could find the time to come to Aber Tidy and open our posh new betting shop.

Should that happen, you might come across grumpy Mansel Morris, and his Garden Village mob. He doesn't like you. He goes round chanting 'Slate loose! Slate loose! Boris has a slate loose!'

But he's the twerp. Take no notice of him. Dai Morgan and I – despite our Labour loyalty – back you big, and that's all that matters.

Truth is, Mansel doesn't like it that all the lovely ladies chase after you. Elsie Morris is the only girlfriend he's had in 50 years, and she wears the thickest specs you'll ever see.

Mansel once said that he'd been mistaken for Tom Cruise, but he didn't say it was by Billy One-eye, and that it was pitch black behind The Elephant in Dumbo Lane.

Fight on, Boris, and don't let those silly burkhas and letter-boxes ruin your life.

Very best wishes,
Cyril Price

Boris Johnson reply

House of Commons,
London.
August 14, 2018.

Hello Cyril,

Thanks so much for your generous support. Our country needs more people like you. It's the only way I am going to lead our Party.

Please 'sell' me discreetly in Doolally Valley, and call me 'Boris the Lion' whenever you wish.

It's time to get Theresa May – or is it May not? – out of the big seat. Her dithering has broken all records.

We happened to stay in the same hotel a few weeks ago and we met in the corridor well after midnight.

She was waving her arms, and snorting. No, not snorting any white stuff. Just snorting.

I asked what was bothering her, and she said she'd spent 15 minutes looking for someone on the night shift, and snapped 'Where is the chambermaid, Boris?'

And, quick as a flash, I replied, "Stoke, I think prime minister. Most are made in the Potteries!"

She went wild, waved her Brexit papers in my face, and chased me to my room, which I locked, and jammed a chair against the door, though I'd have preferred it to be the cabinet! That's supposed to be a joke!

Thanks again, Boris the Lion.

Letter regarding cricketer Ben Stokes

12, Talbot Gardens,
Aber Tidy.
August 23, 2018.

Professor Ed Case,
Psychologist,
Braintree House,
Doolally Valley,
South Wales.

Dear Professor Case,

You will have read in newspapers, or seen on television, the Bristol Crown Court case involving England cricketer Ben Stokes, and the video evidence of him knocking people unconscious in a violent brawl at 2.30 in the morning. He was charged with affray, and acquitted.

During the trial Mr. Stokes admitted to drinking heavily before the ugly fight, which followed an England victory over the West Indies in Bristol.

Cricket is the game I have loved since a child, and I was appalled at Mr. Stokes' outrageous conduct. Indeed, he appears to be a serial offender, having committed a number of disciplinary offences, as well as picking up minor convictions, particularly for speeding.

The big question now is whether he has brought cricket into dispute.

Thank you for your valuable time and advice.
Yours sincerely,
Cyril Price

Psychologist reply

Professor Edward Case,
Braintree House,
Doolally Valley.
August 28, 2018

Dear Mr. Price,

Thank you for contacting me regarding England cricketer, Ben Stokes, who was acquitted of affray at Bristol Crown Court.

Cricket is very much my number one sport. I've played it, and watched it, all over the world, but never been a member of the Barmy Army.

My immediate thought on Ben Stokes is that he might be in the wrong sport.

He has a burning instinct to take up any challenge, is naturally aggressive, and appears to hate losing.
He takes great pride in his performance.

I would like to spend some time talking to Mr. Stokes about his life and ambitions, and assess him closely.

He has made a lot of money from playing cricket, which he does exceptionally well, but I believe he shows all the natural instincts of being a high-class boxer, in which he could make even more money as a champion.

Many of his on-field outbursts appear to come from absolute exasperation. He is bowling a ball when he should be throwing a punch.

Professional athletes have frequently come to me bursting with frustration, and it quickly becomes clear that they are struggling mentally in the wrong sport.

For Ben Stokes it is probably too late to change games, so a weekly workout with a top coach in a boxing club might solve some of his problems. It's definitely worth a try.

Best wishes,

Yours sincerely,
Edward Case

Letter to Nigel Farage

12, Talbot Gardens Aber Tidy,
Doolally Valley,
South Wales.
September 4, 2018.

Dear Mr. Farage,

If it gets out that I've written to you, I'll be fired from the Labour Party, and lose lots of friends, so please keep this contact strictly confidential.

I just had to write to say that your return to front-line politics is profoundly welcomed. You will bring clarity and colour to the Brexit debate.

Theresa doesn't seem to know whether it's May, June or July, and Jeremy Corbyn is a proverbial spinning top.

Our great country needs someone with clear and positive vision for a successful future, and you are just the man to deliver it.

Good luck.

Cyril Price (chairman Aber Tidy Labour Party

12, Talbot Gardens,
Aber Tidy,
Doolally Valley,
South Wales.
October 4, 2018

Lewis Hamilton,
Racing driver,
Mercedes-Benz headquarters,
Stuttgart,
Germany.

Dear Mr. Hamilton,

You are on course to be Formula One champion yet again. Indeed, how can you possibly fail?

You sit in the best car, and when things go wrong your Mercedes colleague, Mr. Bottas, is told to let you go by.

How can anyone say this is a competitive sport? Many teams can barely afford to put a car on the track.

The financial strength of teams between front and back of the grid is immense. And if this is not enough to make a mockery of genuine rivalry, the potential champion is waved to the front when the going gets tough.

To see Mr. Bottas being instructed to give up the lead in last week's Russian Grand Prix was a huge disappointment for the millions of sports people who admire true competition.

If the potential champion jockey was in fourth place in the Derby, can you imagine the first three pulling their horses to one side to let him through? Of course not!
Best of luck, Cyril Price (Top speed 72mph on M4)

12, Talbot Gardens,
Aber Tidy,
Doolally Valley.
October 5, 2018

Reg Phillips,
Secretary,
Conservative Party,
Friar Street,
Aber Tidy.

Dear Reg,

Thank you for writing to report that our new town councillor, Dai ‘twp’ Richards, is harassing Theresa May over Brexit.

Please pass our apologies to the prime minister, and explain that Mr. Richards is the council’s Doolally Valley representative in everything regarding Brexit.

I understand that Mr. Richards is insisting that there should be no hard border with Ireland, which puzzled us at first, as we are hundreds of miles from the coast.

However, we have now discovered that Mr. Richards has a brother in Cardiff, who drives a heavy goods vehicle from his UK base to cities all over Europe.

Mr. Richards is fighting for his brother, who fears long, costly delays while driving to the ports if the hard Irish border becomes part of any Brexit deal.

I’ll have a few more words with him, and assure him that the prime minister is committed to keeping the border open.

Best wishes, Councillor Cyril Price

12, Talbot Gardens,
Aber Tidy,
South Wales.
October 30, 2018.

Angela Merkel,
Chancellor,
Bonn,
Germany.

Dear Angela Merkel,

You are my favourite politician by far. For many years, I have admired your strength and positivity. A supreme leader, who stands her ground, no matter how difficult it might be, and demands absolute justice and fair play.

So your announcement earlier today that you intend to step down in 2021 is a big disappointment for me, though I fully understand that the time has come for you to relax and, maybe, write your memoirs.

Indeed, you may even manage a cruise, and I say beware anyone who dares move your towel from a poolside bed!

I can imagine the 'Iron Freud' carrying the offender on her shoulder, and tipping the idiot over the side.

We have a lovely German lady here in Aber Tidy called Helga Fishlock, who opened the popular Hamburgher Diner in memory of where she went to school.

Anyway, you'll now be well away from that horrendous Putin bloke, who brought a dog to a meeting while knowing you were terribly scared of them after being attacked by one. Enjoy retirement. You deserve it.

Sincerely, Cyril Price

GNOMES VANISH OVERNIGHT

Gnome guard in midnight snatch!

12, Talbot Gardens,
Aber Tidy.
October 31, 2018.

Good morning, Mansel,

Eric Smith woke this morning and found that his three gnomes had vanished from the front lawn. He's greatly upset.

I've just had 30 minutes on the phone with him and Beryl, who said the gnomes were part of the family, and not a day went by without her saying 'good morning' to them.

Eric said he bought them in Holland 20 years ago, and he named them Hans, Knees, and Boompsadaisey. And each one had a specific birthday, which they celebrated, mainly by adding a spot of paint to freshen them up.

I've driven past, and the lawn looks really bare. I know people who actually saluted the gnomes, thinking it would bring them good luck.

So the hunt is on for whoever took them. They didn't walk off, that's for sure, as they were well treated.

I understand that footage from every CCTV camera in the Valley is being scanned, and a large white van, with foreign plates, has shown up leaving the Valley at 4.36 a.m. All ports have been alerted

Eric is sure they weren't gnome sick, and gone back to Holland.

I have wished him the very best of luck, and for a happy gnome-coming!

Interpol traced the gnomes to a boot sale in Bangladesh where light brown shoe polish had altered their complexion to a more appropriate national colour, and they'd been made to look smart in traditional turbans, and given the names Mumbai, Delhi, and Ganges...

Cyril.

LATEST NEWS FROM ABER TIDY

GEORGE, THE GIRAFFE, WINS BY A NECK

Giraffe finishes third but wins by a neck!

+ George, the giraffe, finished third in the Animals Derby, but still won by a neck!

+ Hungry burglar, Nick Silver, has left prison pleading for a full English brexit!

+ Supt. Matthews has revealed that he was appointed head of Aber Tidy police after Supt. Hopkins was sacked for stating that Herr (hair) Dryer was a German General.

+ When asked why he had been standing outside Daisy's Flower shop for more than an hour, Dai 'twp' Richards pointed to the sign that said 'Please mind the step'.

+ Aber Tidy's new mayor is insisting he's not a chain smoker

....

www.ingramcontent.com/pod-product-compliance
Ingram Content Group UK Ltd.
Pitfield, Milton Keynes, MK11 3LW, UK
UKHW041844200726
13854UKWH00005BA/2054

9 781789 554526